For Audrey, with love

The Butter Battle Book

By Dr. Seuss

RANDOM HOUSE NEW YORK

Library of Congress Cataloging in Publication Data:
Seuss, Dr. The butter battle book. SUMMARY: Engaged in a long-running battle, the Yooks and the Zooks develop more and more sophisticated weaponry as they attempt to outdo each other. [1. War–Fiction. 2. Stories in rhyme] I. Title. PZ8.3.G276Bu 1984 [Fic] 83-21286 ISBN: 0-394-86580-4 (trade); 0-394-96580-9 (lib. bdg.); 0-394-86716-5 (ltd. ed.)

Manufactured in the United States of America   1 2 3 4 5 6 7 8 9 0

On the last day of summer,
ten hours before fall . . .

. . . my grandfather took me
out to the Wall.

For a while he stood silent.
Then finally he said,
with a very sad shake
of his very old head,
"As you know, on this side of the Wall
we are Yooks.
On the far other side of this Wall
live the Zooks."

Then my grandfather said,
"It's high time that you knew
of the terribly horrible thing that Zooks do.
In every Zook house and in every Zook town
*every Zook eats his bread
with the butter side down!*

"But we Yooks, as you know,
when we breakfast or sup,
spread our bread," Grandpa said,
"with the butter side *up*.
That's the right, honest way!"
Grandpa gritted his teeth.
"So you can't trust a Zook who spreads bread underneath!
Every Zook must be watched!
He has kinks in his soul!
That's why, as a youth, I made watching my goal,
watching Zooks for the Zook-Watching Border Patrol!

In those days, of course,
the Wall wasn't so high
and I could look any Zook
square in the eye.

If he dared to come close
I could give him a twitch
with my tough-tufted
prickely Snick-Berry Switch.

For a while that worked fine.
All the Zooks stayed away
and our country was safe.
Then one terrible day
a very rude Zook by the name of VanItch
snuck up and slingshotted my Snick-Berry Switch!

With my broken-off switch, with my head hung in shame,
to the Chief Yookeroo in great sorrow I came.
But our Leader just smiled. He said, "You're not to blame.
And those Zooks will be sorry they started this game.

"We'll dress you right up in a fancier suit!
We'll give you a fancier slingshot to shoot!"
And he ordered the Boys in the Back Room to figger
how to build me some sort of a triple-sling jigger.

With my Triple-Sling Jigger
I sure felt much bigger.

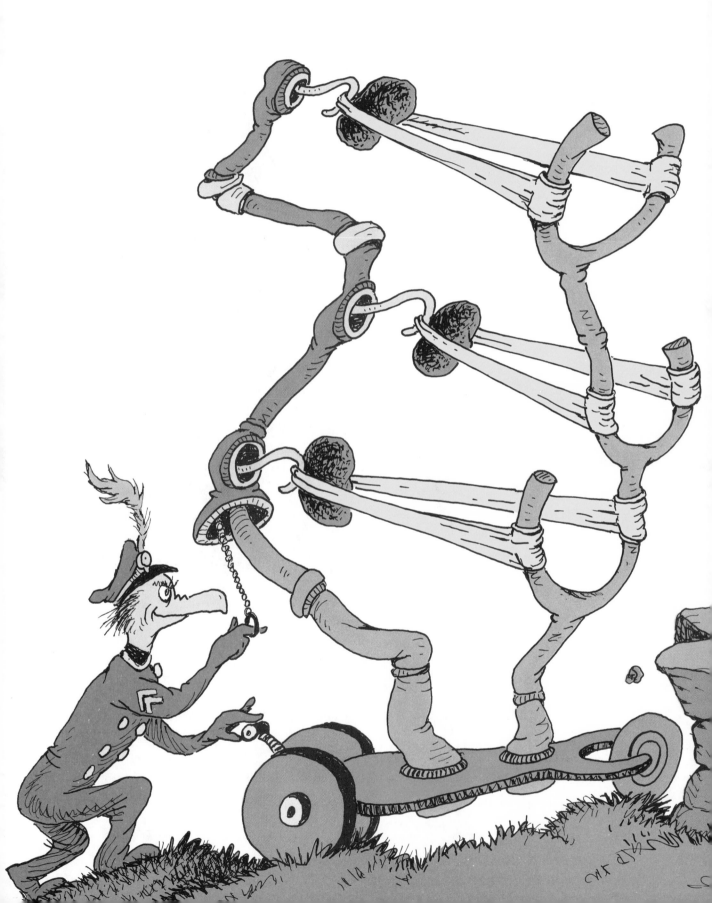

I marched to the Wall with great vim and great vigor,
right up to VanItch with my hand on the trigger.
"I'll have no more nonsense," I said with a frown,
"from Zooks who eat bread with the butter side down!"

VanItch looked quite sickly.
He ran off quite quickly.

I'm unhappy to say
he came back the next day
in a spiffy new suit with a big new machine,
and he snarled as he said, looking frightfully mean,
"You may fling those hard rocks with your Triple-Sling Jigger.
But I, also, now have *my* hand on a trigger!

"My wonderful weapon, the Jigger-Rock Snatchem,
will fling 'em right back just as quick as we catch 'em.
We'll have no more nonsense.
We'll take no more gupp
from you Yooks who eat bread with the butter side up!"

"I have failed, sir," I sobbed as I made my report
to the Chief Yookeroo in the headquarters fort.
He just laughed. "You've done nothing at all of the sort.
                    Our slingshots have failed.
                    That was old-fashioned stuff.
                    Slingshots, dear boy,
                    are not modern enough.

"All we need is some newfangled kind of a gun.
My Boys in the Back Room have already begun
to think up a walloping whizz-zinger one!
My Bright Boys are thinking.
They're on the right track.
They'll think one up quick
and we'll send you right back!"

They thought up a great one!
They certainly did.
They thought up a gun called the Kick-a-Poo Kid
which they loaded with powerful Poo-a-Doo Powder
and ants' eggs and bees' legs
and dried-fried clam chowder.
And they carefully trained a real smart dog named Daniel
to serve as our country's first gun-toting spaniel.

Then Daniel, the Kick-a-Poo Spaniel, and I
marched back toward the Wall
with our heads held up high
while everyone cheered and their cheers filled the sky:
"Fight! Fight for the Butter Side Up!
Do or die!"

Well . . .
We didn't *do*.
And we didn't quite die.
But we sure did get worsted, poor Daniel and I.
VanItch was there too! And he said, the old pig,
"The Boys in *my* Back Room invented *this* rig
called the Eight-Nozzled, Elephant-Toted Boom-Blitz.
It shoots high-explosive sour cherry stone pits
and will put your dumb Kick-a-Poo Kid on the fritz!"
      Poor Daniel and I
      were scared out of our witz!

Once more, by VanItch I was bested and beat.
Once again I limped home from the Wall in defeat.
I dragged and I sagged
and my spirits were low,
as low as I thought that they ever could go,
when I heard a *Boom-Bah!*
And a *Diddle-dee-Dill!*
And our Butter-Up Band
marched up over the hill!

The Chief Yookeroo had sent them to meet me
along with the Right-Side-Up Song Girls to greet me.
They sang:

> "Oh, be faithful!
> Believe in thy butter!"

And they lifted my spirits right out of the gutter!

"My boy," smiled the Chief Yookeroo, "we've just voted
and made you a general! You've been promoted.
Your pretty new uniform's ready. Get in it!
The Big War is coming. You're going to begin it!
And what's more, *this* time you are certain to win it.

"My Boys in the Back Room have finally found how.
Just wait till you see what they've puttered up now!
In their great new machine you'll fly over that Wall
and clobber those Butter-Down Zooks one and all!"

Those Boys in the Back Room sure knew how to putter!
They made me a thing called the Utterly Sputter
and I jumped aboard with my heart all aflutter
and steered toward the land
of the Upside-Down Butter.

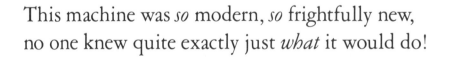

This machine was *so* modern, *so* frightfully new,
no one knew quite exactly just *what* it would do!

But it had several faucets that sprinkled Blue Goo
which, somehow, would sprinkle the Zooks as I flew
and gum up that upside-down butter they chew.

I was racing pell-mell
when I heard a voice yell,
"If you sprinkle us Zooks,
you'll get sprinkled as well!"

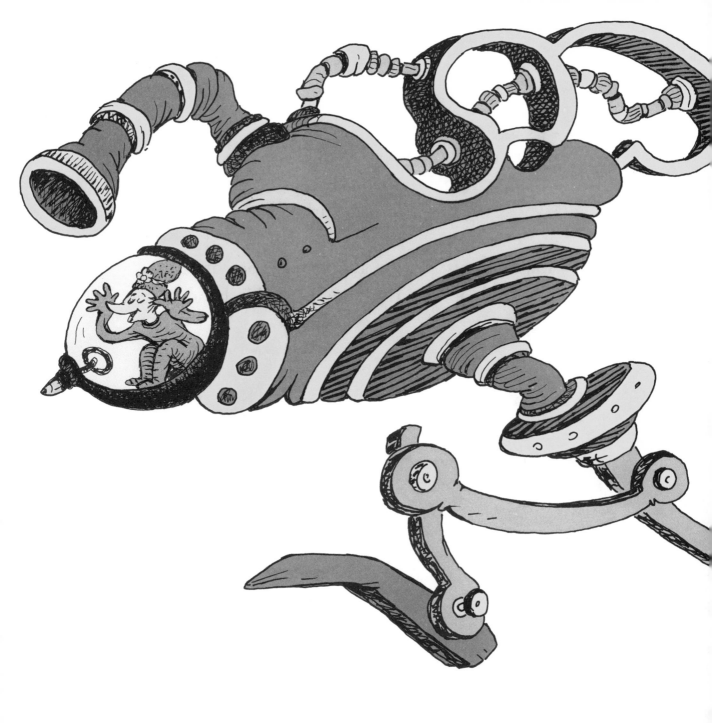

VanItch had a Sputter exactly like mine!
And he yelled, "My Blue-Gooer is working just fine!
And I'm here to say that if Yooks can goo Zooks,
you'd better forget it. 'Cause Zooks can goo Yooks!"

I flew right back home
and, as you may have guessed,
I was downright despondent,
                    disturbed,
                              and depressed.
And I saw, just as soon as I stepped back on land,
so were all of the girls of the Butter-Up Band.

The Chief Drum Majorette, Miz Yookie-Ann Sue,
said, "That was a pretty sour flight that you flew.
And the Chief Yookeroo has been looking for you!"

I raced to his office. The place was a sight.
"Have no fears," said the Chief. "Everything is all right.
My Bright Back Room Boys have been brighter than bright.
They've thought up a gadget that's Newer than New.
It is filled with mysterious Moo-Lacka-Moo
and can blow all those Zooks clear to Sala-ma-goo.
THEY'VE INVENTED
                    THE BITSY
                              BIG-BOY BOOMEROO!

"You just run to the wall like a nice little man.
Drop this bomb on the Zooks just as fast as you can.
I have ordered all Yooks to stay safe underground
while the Bitsy Big-Boy Boomeroo is around."

As I raced for that Wall, with the bomb in my hand,
I noticed that every last Yook in our land
was obeying our Chief Yookeroo's grim command.

They were all bravely marching,
with banners aflutter,
down a hole! For their country!
And Right-Side-Up Butter!

That's when Grandfather found me!
He grabbed me. He said,
     "You should be down that hole!
     And you're up here instead!
     But perhaps this is all for the better, somehow.
     You will see me make history!
     RIGHT HERE! AND RIGHT NOW!"

Grandpa leapt up that Wall with a lopulous leap
and he cleared his hoarse throat
with a bopulous beep.
He screamed, "Here's the end of that terrible town
full of Zooks who eat bread with the butter side down!"

And at that very instant we heard a klupp-klupp
of feet on the Wall and old VanItch klupped up!
The Boys in HIS Back Room had made him one too!
In his fist was another Big-Boy Boomeroo!
"I'll blow you," he yelled, "into pork and wee beans!
I'll butter-side-up you to small smithereens!"

"Grandpa!" I shouted. "Be careful! Oh, gee!
Who's going to drop it?
Will *you*...? Or will *he*...?"
"Be patient," said Grandpa. "We'll see.
We will see..."